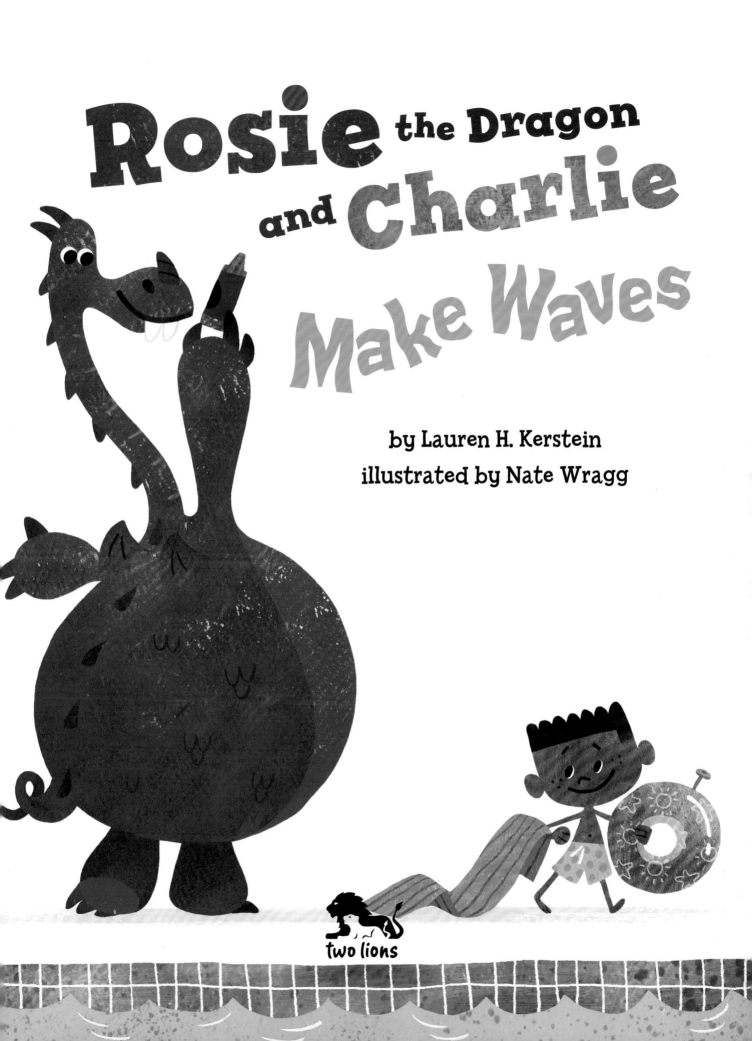

Rosie the Dragon and Charlie Make Waves

by Lauren H. Kerstein

illustrated by Nate Wragg

two lions

For Sarah, Danielle, and Josh. Dreams do come true!
—L. H. K.

For my dad. Thank you for making waves with me, too!
—N. W.

Published by Two Lions, New York

www.apub.com

Amazon, the Amazon logo, and Two Lions are
trademarks of Amazon.com, Inc., or its affiliates.

ISBN-13: 9781542042925 (hardcover)
ISBN-10: 1542042925 (hardcover)

The illustrations are rendered in digital media.
Book design by Tanya Ross-Hughes

Printed in China

First Edition

10 9 8 7 6 5 4 3 2 1

Hi! I'm Charlie.
This is Rosie.

Rosie?
Rosie!

Don't stick out your tongue.
Just. Say. Hi.

Geesh! Sorry about that.

I didn't plan to adopt a dragon, but Rosie found me irresistible.
I think she liked my skunk hat.

And now we're best friends.
We do everything together.

Today we're heading to the pool. Rosie wants to practice swimming.

Our last pool outing didn't go that well, so I stayed up
all night preparing. Today will be terrific!

Before we leave, Rosie searches for swim gear.
Don't worry, she'll choose some . . . eventually.

Then we apply sunblock. Everywhere.
Rosie, wait! I'm not finished!

Last, we fill our bag with supplies. I like preparing for all pool possibilities. I even pack gummy skunks for **AFTER** swimming. Rosie loves them, but they cause **BLUE** teeth and—*SHUDDER*—wicked dragon breath.

Last week when she ate them
at the bowling alley, they sparked
a few . . . er . . . problems!

Okay, Rosie, let's go to the pool!

Finally, we arrive at the pool.
Rosie races toward the water.

Wait! This time,
let's review the rules
before you leap in.

≈ RULES ≈

RULE #1: No drinking. Pool water is not a beverage.

RULE #2: No running. We don't want another cracked-cement catastrophe.

RULE #3: No diving. Or belly flops. Safety comes first.

Okay, Rosie, let's play.
She snaps on her cap and plops into the water.

Sharing isn't easy for a dragon,
even with friends, so I keep extra
toys handy. *Rosie! That's not yours.*

I ask Rosie to eat her knight-shaped cookies in private, in case she bites off the head. It's disturbing. **YIKES!**

KNIGHT SNACKS

Rosie, let's eat some cool snacks instead!
I'm ready! Dig in!

Uh-oh! Rosie is eyeing the gummy skunks.
Rosie, NO! Remember, those are an after-swim snack.
I hide them and . . .

tug . . . I mean *lead* Rosie away.
No more snacks.
Let's blow bubbles.

Rosie loves bubbles. The bigger, the better. But sometimes her bubbles grow a little *too* big. So today we're practicing in the baby pool.

Rosie, just lean your face into the water.
I put on a raincoat and offer umbrellas
to small children . . .

but they are no match for Rosie's colossal bubbles.
Rosie! Let's practice flutter kicks
in the big pool . . . NOW!

Rosie dashes into the water and hangs on to the wall.
She FLUTTERS . . . FLUTTERS . . . **FLUTTERS.**

Parents clutch children.
Swimmers scream.
Lifeguards leap.

Okay, Rosie, that's enough!

Sorry, everyone!

I steer **Rosie** away and help her calm down.
It's okay. Let's try a shoulder ride.

Dragon breath can be a bit . . . um . . . fiery! So I clip on Rosie's nose plug. Rosie kicks . . . **kicks** . . . *Gently, Rosie* . . . kicks.

The ride is bumpy, but we're making progress. We whirl around and around and around, picking up a few friends along the way.

Thirty laps later,
I decide we're ready
for a challenge.
Rosie, let's swim to the wall.

Okay, Rosie, extend your arms.
1-2-3 a-a-a-a-and . . . GO!

Rosie dragon-paddles, pants, and shoots sparks across the pool.

Put your face in the water. Blow bubbles, not sparks!
Much better!

We rest for a second.

You know what, Rosie? I think you're ready to swim by yourself.

Her nostrils flare. *Wait! Don't run away.*
I quickly reassure her with a few last tips.
Flames flicker sometimes. You'll find your fire again.
Kick gently and you'll avoid another tidal wave.
I know the lifeguards look concerned.
They just want to help.

You've got this, Rosie.
Rosie winks.

a-a-a-a-and plunges in!

Hurray!
Rosie is swimming with friends.
I snap pictures for our photo al—

Sniff. Sniff. Sniff.
OH NO!

What a day! While they refill the pool (and fix toppled tables and chairs), Rosie and I snuggle to read books with friends.

Rosie can't wait to learn
how to read.

flash

sizzle

Reading
for
Dragons

GULP! *It's okay, Rosie. We'll learn together.*